W9-AWU-942

# THE PIRATE AND THE PRINCESS

## The Timelight Stone

Originally entitled in Japanese:
"Shoujo Kaizoku Yuri – Nazo No Jikouseki"
Text copyright © 2001 by Chizuru Mio
Illustrations copyright © 2001 by Ayako Nagamori
First published in Japan in 2001 by
DOSHINSHA Publishing Co., Ltd.
English translation rights arranged with DOSHINSHA
Publishing Co., Ltd. through Japan Foreign-Rights Centre

All rights reserved. No part of this book may be reproduced or
transmitted in any form or by any means, electronic or mechanical,
including photocopying, recording, or by any information storage
and retrieval system, without written permission from
the publisher, except where permitted by law.

Published by Seven Seas Entertainment, LLC.
Cover and interior design by Two Red Shoes Design

ISBN: 978-1-933164-43-4
Printed in Canada

# THE PIRATE AND THE PRINCESS

## The Timelight Stone

Written by
MIO CHIZURU

Illustrations by Ayako Nagamori
Adapted by Tracey West

Seven Seas

LOS ANGELES

# The Pirate Ship Eurastia

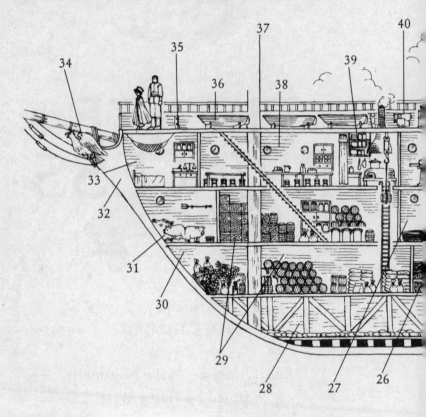

1. Main mast
2. Quarterdeck
3. Time Bell
4. Meeting Space
5. Repair Space
6. Library
7. Mizzenmast
8. Pilothouse
9. Upper Quarterdeck (Poop Deck)
10. Workshop

11. Tactics
12. Captain's Cabin
13. Captain's Lounge
14. Experiments
15. Rudder
16. Livestock
17. Weapons Armory
18. Karazan's Cabin
19. Break Space
20. Treasure Hold

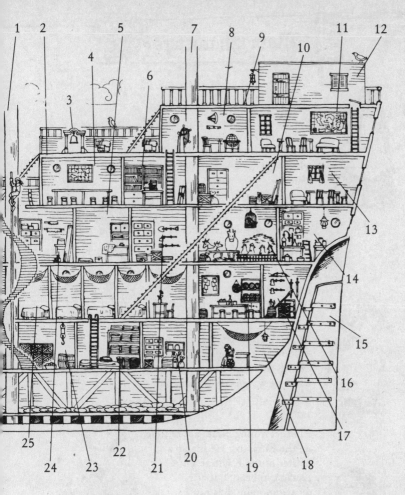

1  2  5  7  8  9  10  11  12
4  6
3

13

14

15

16

17

25  24  23  22  21  20  19  18

# Main Characters

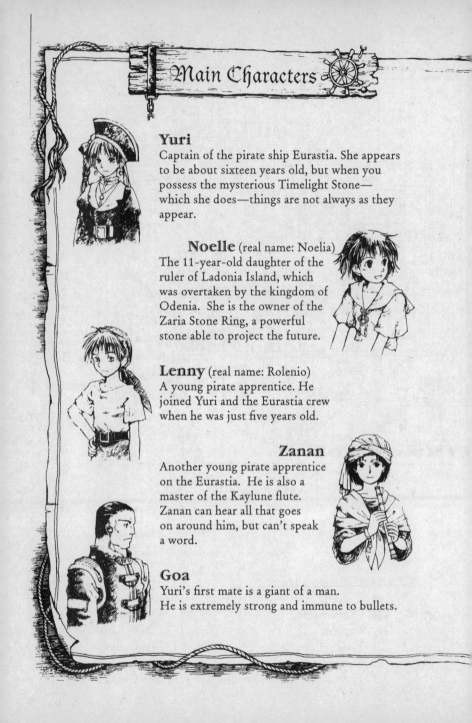

### Yuri
Captain of the pirate ship Eurastia. She appears to be about sixteen years old, but when you possess the mysterious Timelight Stone—which she does—things are not always as they appear.

### Noelle (real name: Noelia)
The 11-year-old daughter of the ruler of Ladonia Island, which was overtaken by the kingdom of Odenia. She is the owner of the Zaria Stone Ring, a powerful stone able to project the future.

### Lenny (real name: Rolenio)
A young pirate apprentice. He joined Yuri and the Eurastia crew when he was just five years old.

### Zanan
Another young pirate apprentice on the Eurastia. He is also a master of the Kaylune flute. Zanan can hear all that goes on around him, but can't speak a word.

### Goa
Yuri's first mate is a giant of a man. He is extremely strong and immune to bullets.

## Pipps

The great merchant of Odenia. This corrupt
man will do anything for money.

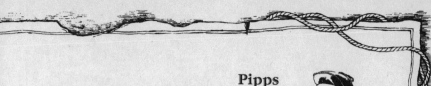

### King Roden

He rules the kingdom
of Odenia, but the one
thing he wants the most
he can't seem to get: the
Zaria Stone Ring.

### Black Cloak

A mysterious man. He knows Yuri's secret
and wants the Timelight Stone.

### Majobaba

A healer who lives on Pirate's Wharf. She aids
Yuri with love and understanding.

### Karazan

A 101 year-old pirate on the Eurastia. He is known as Karazan
the Prophet.

### General Datton

Head of the Odenian Navy. A devoted general, he is pledged
to help King Roden find the Zaria Stone Ring.

# Prologue

Afternoon sunlight glimmered on the ocean waves. Yuri stood on the main deck of her pirate ship, gazing out onto the horizon. On a clear day like this, it seemed as though she could see to the ends of the earth.

A light wind fluttered through the blue cloak that Yuri wore around her shoulders. The sun shone on her braided, golden brown hair, which streamed out from under her red three-cornered hat. Her face had the youthful appearance of a six-teen-year-old girl. But the look in her dark eyes was one of a person who had lived far, far longer.

The sound of heavy footsteps creaked on the deck's wooden planks. Goa, her first mate, came up beside her. A giant of a man, Goa towered over Yuri. His rugged face looked like it had been carved out of stone. The brass buttons on his red jacket gleamed with polish.

"Lunch is ready," he announced. "Will you eat in the Captain's Cabin?"

Yuri continued to stare at the sea. "Goa, how long have we been sailing these waters?" she asked quietly.

"Today will make two hundred and two years, five months, and ten days," Goa replied.

Yuri reached for the gold locket she wore around her neck. She opened the lid. Inside was a round, blue stone. The color reminded Yuri of bright, tropical waters, or the feathers of an exotic bird. She lightly touched the stone with her fingertips.

"How long must we carry this stone?" She

wondered out loud. "How long must we sail the seas?"

As if in answer to her question, a blue light glowed from the heart of the stone. Yuri gasped. The stone had been in her possession for many years, but its strange powers never stopped amazing her.

The blue light grew stronger, exploding from the stone in a wide beam. Yuri watched as the stone seemed to rip a hole in time and space right in front of her eyes. She was no longer looking out at the sunny sky. Instead, she saw a vast, dark ocean. A black ship sailed over the waves, silhouetted against a gloomy sky.

Then a voice came through the light.

*Help . . . .*

Yuri could barely hear the cry. It sounded like it was being drowned out by a strong wind. But the plea for help came through. And it was desperate.

The light flashed and then vanished. Yuri was looking out at the blue waves once again. She closed the locket. Then she turned and faced Goa.

"What is the ship's position?" she asked.

"We're in the middle of the Lidenia Sea, sailing southwest at fifteen knots," Goa replied.

"We need to change course," Yuri said quickly. It was difficult to describe, even after all this time, but her connection to the stone ran deep. She knew exactly where they would find the black ship, where the cry for help had come from. "Bring the ship around on an easterly heading."

Goa frowned slightly. "But we need to replenish our supplies at Pirate's Wharf—"

Yuri cut him off. "We'll do that later, Goa," she said firmly. "Someone's calling for help. We might be too late."

Goa nodded. "I understand, Captain Yuri." The large man saluted and then quickly turned and walked away.

Yuri looked back out at the ship's rail. It didn't take long for them to change direction. Soon she gazed out over the Eastern sky. The light wind grew stronger, feeling cool on her skin.

There wasn't a cloud in the blue sky ahead, but Yuri knew a storm was coming. She could feel it in her bones.

"Just hang on a little longer," she softly called across the waves. "We'll be there soon."

# Chapter One:
# Noelle

Deep in the hold of the black ship, a young girl huddled in the corner. Around her, other captives slept fitfully. Their clothes were ragged and torn; their faces dirty with dust and grime.

Something brushed past her ankle, and Noelle shivered.

*Probably a rat*, she knew, but tried not to think about it. She had encountered a lot worse than rats in the last week of her life. She closed her eyes and tried to sleep. Thoughts raced through her mind. She tried to block them out, but hot tears stung her eyes. Noelle angrily brushed them away.

*Tears won't help you now*, she scolded herself. *Sleep, sleep so you can be strong. So you can get out of here . . .*

Then the ship groaned suddenly. Noelle could tell they were in shallow waters. A dim light appeared in the hold, and a man's voice barked, "Time to get up! Don't be lazy! Get a move on!"

The captives moved in silent confusion, walking up the ladder to the ship's weather deck. The chilly night air shocked Noelle for a second but she gulped it in gratefully. It was the freshest air she had breathed for days.

She looked around, trying to get her bearings. The ship had docked in some kind of harbor. Noelle squinted, looking for a village, some friendly faces, some hope of escape. But only dark rocks ringed the inlet and Noelle couldn't see beyond them.

The sailors herded the captives down the

gangplank. Noelle saw a fat man standing down below. His long cloak was trimmed with expensive fur. A gold watch on a chain hung from his jacket pocket and he smoked a pipe. The smoke wafted up to his thin, curled mustache.

A tall, skinny man Noelle recognized as the captain of the ship walked up to him. The two men began to talk.

Noelle wondered what they were talking about. If her fate rested in the hands of that frightening-looking man, she'd prefer to be left with the rats.

The ship's captain paraded the captives in front of the fat man one by one. When it was her turn, Noelle glared at the man, staring into his beady eyes.

"I'm Pipps," the portly man said gruffly. "Tell me your name, girl."

Noelle refused to answer.

The ship's captain tugged hard on her arm. "Answer the man!"

The jolt sent something flying out of her pocket. It tumbled to the ground. Noelle tried to reach for it, but Pipps was faster.

Pipps held the shiny object up to his face. It was a gold ring set with a blood red, round jewel in the center. Deep inside the stone, a white light shone like a star.

"Give it back!" Noelle shouted, angry and scared.

Pipps' dark eyes gleamed as he looked at the ring. He smiled.

"Can it be?" he asked softly. Then he turned to the captain.

"Where was this girl captured?" he asked.

The captain scratched his head thoughtfully. "We caught her roaming the streets of Cretas Island," he answered after a moment.

Pipps' eyes lit up. "Cretas Island is right next to Ladonia Island, isn't it?" he asked. He looked at Noelle, and his lips curled into a snake-like smile. "That's funny, because this looks like the Ladonian hidden treasure to me—the Zaria Stone Ring!'

Noelle's body stiffened. Every cell in her body wanted to leap at the man, to grab the ring and run, just run. But she had to be smarter than that.

Pipps gazed at the ring. "According to the

legend, a red stone fell from the sky and landed in Ladonia. They say the stone possesses the light of a star. When you expose it to the light of the moon, this miraculous stone can see into the future!"

Noelle looked to her left, to her right. Pipps was too close to the truth now. She had to find some way to get the ring back, and escape . . .

"The ruler of Ladonia has passed down the Zaria Stone Ring from generation to generation," Pipps went on. "With the power of the ring, the kingdom of Ladonia had never lost in battle. Until last week, that is, when at last Ladonia fell to the power of the Odenian army."

Noelle felt herself trembling at the memory. It had all happened so quickly . . . .

Pipps turned his snarly gaze to Noelle. "The ruler of Ladonia and his wife perished. But it is reported that their child went missing, along with the Zaria Stone Ring. In fact, they've promised a five hundred thousand diran reward to anyone who brings in the girl."

The fat man took a step closer. "The child is an eleven year old girl with blue eyes. Her name . . . is Noelle."

So Pipps had discovered her secret. Noelle knew she had to act. Swiftly, she used her elbow to jab the skinny captain hard in the ribs.

"Ow!" he wailed.

Then she ran—right into two men, thugs who worked for Pipps. The men each grabbed one of her arms and dragged her back in front of Pipps. She tried to dig her bare feet into the rocky sand, but it was no use.

"Let me go!" she cried.

Pipps let out a deep laugh. "I am a lucky man today! Who would have guessed this ship would bring me a child worth five hundred thousand diran?"

Noelle had never felt so helpless—or so angry. "I hope the Eurastia comes to destroy you!" she shouted, her body shaking.

Pipps grinned. "The Eurastia? You mean the legendary pirate ship?"

"That's right," Noelle said. "The Eurastia answers the prayers of people in trouble and comes to punish the bad guys. My nurse told me all about it. I know the Eurastia will come save me!"

The sailors burst into laughter. Pipps joined them, his big belly shaking.

"Is that so?" Pipps asked. "Well, you keep on wishing all you want."

Noelle's fists clenched. Maybe the Eurastia was only a bedtime story but it was all she had. Trapped in the hold of the ship, she had quietly called out to Yuri, the pirate captain of the Eurastia. The idea that someone, somewhere, might be able to save her had seen her through the long days and nights.

Pipps nodded to the thugs, his face once again serious. "Lock her up."

"You got it, boss," one of the men said gruffly.

Noelle tried to pull herself out of their grasp. "I won't go!" she yelled. "I won't—"

BOOM!

The deafening sound came from the Black Ship. Noelle turned to see the ship's tall, wood mast exploding into pieces. The burning pieces struck the ship's black sails as they fell. In seconds, the sails burned with angry orange flames.

## Chapter Two:
# Siege of the Black Ship

Stunned, Pipps stared at the burning ship.

"What is going on?" he asked.

The answer came in a loud cry from the shore-line. Several rowboats—too many for Noelle to count—sped toward the harbor. Each boat held three or four men. They waved long, curved swords in the air.

Chaos erupted on the shore. The men jumped

out of the boats, charged toward the sailors and Pipps' men. The thugs and the Black Ship sailors were mostly armed with daggers and knives. Some of them ran toward the attackers, weapons drawn, while others fled in fear.

For the first time in a week, a glimmer of hope sprang in Noelle's heart. The attackers looked like . . . pirates. But could it be? It was too much to ask for.

One of the thugs nodded at Pipps. "Sir, it's dangerous here. You must escape!"

"What are you saying?" Pipps growled. "We can't let them take what is ours!"

But the attackers swarmed the shore, cutting down any opponent in their path. Their swords were no match for the sailors' puny weapons.

Pipps' face turned red with anger. "Confound it! At least grab the girl. She's worth five hundred thousand diran!"

The other thug grabbed Noelle. She kicked and screamed in protest. Pipps quickly hurried away from the inlet.

The spark of hope died in Noelle. Pipps prob-

ably had a secret ship stashed somewhere. All of the other captives would be freed, except for her.

"Help!" she screamed, hoping one of the pirates would hear her. But they were far from the fray now. She hung her head, lost in despair.

Suddenly, Pipps stopped. Noelle looked up. A torch burned on the path just ahead.

"You still haven't learned, have you, Pipps?"

The voice was soft but firm. The torch-bearing figure walked closer, and Noelle saw the person was wearing a blue cloak that covered their head and face.

Beside Noelle, Pipps turned as pale as milk.

"It's . . . it's you . . ." he stammered.

"You promised me, Pipps," said the figure. "You promised me you would stop making money from the lives of innocent people. I saved your life but you broke your promise anyway, didn't you?"

The cloaked figure moved closer to Pipps. She lowered her hood to reveal the face of a sixteen-year-old girl with golden brown hair.

It was Yuri. Goa stood behind her.

Noelle gasped. The girl looked just like she had

imagined Yuri, the pirate captain, would look.
Could the stories be true?

Pipps looked terrified. "Yuri, why are you
here?"

"I heard it," Yuri said. She nodded at Noelle. "I
heard her call for help."

"So, are you . . ." Noelle's voice trailed off
weakly.

"Yuri of the Eurastia," she replied. She glared
at the thug holding Noelle. "Let go of the child
now."

The other thug started to draw his sword, but
Pipps quickly stopped him.

"Fool!" he cried. "Don't you know how good
this woman is with a sword? Let the girl go."

The thug loosened his grip on Noelle, who
quickly ran to Yuri's side. Yuri smiled. She drew
her sword and leveled it at Pipps' nose.

"You're a clever man, Pipps," she said. "Since
you're clever, I know you'll return to this girl
what you stole from her."

Pipps groaned quietly and dug into his pocket.
He handed the ring to Noelle and she swiftly

grabbed it from his thick fingers.

Yuri looked surprised at the sight of the ring. She stared intently at Noelle for a moment. Then she turned to Pipps, giving him a stern look.

"Promise me again, Pipps," she said. "Promise me you won't deal in captives anymore."

Pipps looked down at the sword pointed at his nose.

"I promise . . . not to do it again," he answered through gritted teeth.

Yuri's wrist made two impossibly fast movements. Pipps cried out in shock as his mustache suddenly fell off his face, and floated down to the ground.

"I'll take your promise as proof of your pledge," Yuri told him. "If you dare forget, next time it'll be more than your mustache."

Yuri lowered her sword. Pipps made no response, but his eyes were a mirror of his fear.

Yuri grabbed Noelle's hand.

"Come," she said. "The night is cold."

Yuri led her back to the harbor. Her men were leading Noelle's fellow captives to the safety of the rowboats. The burning black ship was sinking into the waters.

Yuri helped Noelle climb into a boat. Goa climbed in next and manned the oars. Soon the rowboat was gliding over the waves.

"We'll get back to the ship quickly and warm up," Yuri assured her. She draped her blue cloak over Noelle's shivering shoulders.

"Ship?" Noelle asked. "Is it really—"

"The Eurastia," Yuri answered.

Noelle looked past Yuri into the dark ocean. In

the distance, a large sailing ship bobbed on top of the waves.

"The Eurastia," Noelle whispered. She felt like she was in a dream. But the warm cloak, the rocking waves, the sound of Yuri's soft breathing—it was all real. She had called out for help, and Yuri had heard her.

Exhausted, Noelle closed her eyes and fell into a deep sleep.

Chapter Three:
# The Eurastia

Noelle opened her eyes. She was on the deck of a ship. The brilliant morning sun shone overhead.

She shielded her eyes and squinted. Where was she, exactly? Then two figures appeared on the deck and walked toward her. Noelle lit up like a Christmas tree.

"Mother! Father!" she cried.

She ran toward her parents with open arms.

Her little brother, Johann, toddled behind them. Noelle couldn't wait to hug them all again, to hold them.

But suddenly she felt as though she couldn't move. Someone had grabbed her arms, pinning them behind her. She turned to see Griffith, a trusted member of her father's court. His face was twisted in an evil grin.

"Let me go!" Noelle cried. But she could not free herself from his grasp.

In the distance, her mother, father, and Johann began to move backward, as though pulled by a magnet, some unseen force.

"Don't go!" Noelle screamed. "Mother! Father! Wait!"

"Miss Noelle, are you okay?"

Noelle opened her eyes—for real, this time.

It had all been a dream.

She looked up into the concerned face of Goa. At another time, in other circumstances, the craggy face of the large man might have scared her. But she only saw kindness in his eyes.

He gently placed his hand on her forehead.

Then he smiled with relief.

"Thank goodness," he said. "Your fever has died down. Some food is on the way."

Noelle looked around and saw she was actually inside the boat, in a small ship's cabin. Sunlight shone in through one lone, round, porthole. She realized she was lying in a hammock. The sheets on top of her smelled of fresh air and ocean waves. Next to the hammock was a small wood table. A round clay pot held a bunch of colorful flowers.

The events of the night before came flooding back to her.

*I'm in the Eurastia*, she realized. *The legendary ship. And Yuri the pirate captain—Yuri saved me.*

"The fever struck as soon as we got you on board," Goa explained. "You've been tossing and turning all night."

There was a knock on the door. Before Goa could answer, the door swung open, and a young boy came in, carrying a tray of food. The boy looked to be about Noelle's age. His eyes were clear green and his smooth hair was a light, golden blond.

"Goa, I brought the food," the boy announced.

Noelle gave him a weak smile, but the boy seemed quite annoyed. He didn't smile in return.

The boy placed the tray on the table. Noelle had a million questions she wanted to ask but the smell of the food completely took over her senses. She climbed out of the hammock and noticed, with relief, that her filthy clothes had been replaced with a clean blouse and skirt. Then she sat down at the table.

The tray held a plate of sizzling bacon. There

was a wicker basket filled with warm bread, butter, and hunks of cheese. Steam puffed up from a round bowl, and Noelle looked inside to see a hearty bean soup.

Suddenly she was hungrier than she had ever been in her life. She swallowed a chunk of bread nearly whole. She left the spoon on the table and picked up the soup bowl with both hands, downing it in just a few gulps. Then she devoured the bacon and cheese.

The boy stared at Noelle in disbelief. "Amazing," he said.

Goa laughed. "If you can eat like that, then we have nothing to worry about. It would be good if you got some fresh air, though."

He turned to the boy. "Lenny, show Noelle around. I'll clean up here."

The boy scowled. He roughly grabbed Noelle's hand. "Follow me," he said.

Noelle looked longingly at some crumbs of cheese left on the plate, but the boy dragged her off. When they went through the door, Lenny dropped her hand and marched quickly ahead of her.

"Wait!" Noelle cried. "Can we walk a little slower, please? Hey, you—"

The boy turned sharply. "My name is Rolenio, but people call me Lenny," he snapped. "I'm a pirate apprentice, so you'd better not mess around with me. I've been on this ship since I was five. Not a single person on the Eurastia can climb the mast better than me!"

"Oh really?" Noelle replied, putting her hands on her hips. "My name is Noelia, but people call me Noelle. I may look small but I know how to use a sword. So don't mess with me, either!"

Lenny's face was blank for a moment. Then he broke into a grin.

"That's a relief," he said. "I thought you were some princess type or something who'd want to be waited on hand and foot. But I guess you're just a regular girl."

He held out his hand, and Noelle shook it.

"Uh, nice to meet you," she said. She wasn't sure what to make of this boy.

He nodded. "Come on, I'll show you around the ship. Let's start with the deck!"

Lenny started to run down the passage.

"Hey, slow down!" Noelle called out.

Her legs were weak from the fever and from being in the cramped hold on the black ship for so long. But Lenny's excitement was contagious. She ran after him as fast as she could. They climbed a ladder, scurried down another passage, climbed some stairs, and then, finally, Lenny opened a hatch above them.

Noelle followed him out onto the deck. The bright sunlight nearly blinded her. A fresh sea breeze blew against her face. She ran to the rails and looked out. Pure white clouds drifted over the deep blue sea. There was nothing between the sea and the sky but the white sails of the Eurastia.

Was this a dream, too? She gripped the rails tightly, feeling the rough worn wood under her palms. A spray of cold water tickled her cheek. The sun warmed her bare arms.

It was real.

"I'm really here," she said, half whispering. "I'm on the Eurastia."

Lenny walked to her side. "What are you talking

about? What did you expect?"

"My nurse used to tell me stories about the Eurastia every night before I fell asleep," Noelle explained. "Once she told me how the Eurastia plunged into the middle of a storm to save a wrecked ship. And she said the captain summoned a hurricane to escape the Odenian navy."

Lenny's green eyes widened.

"She said that everyone on the Eurastia is incredibly brave, and that the ship's captain has been alive for three hundred years," Noelle went on. "So you see, it all seems a little unreal. I feel like I'm in the middle of one of my nurse's stories."

Lenny looked embarrassed. "So, those are the stories they tell about us, huh?" he asked, scratching his head.

But Noelle was lost in her thoughts again. She gazed around the ship. Huge white sails billowed on the mast. There were three more decks stacked above them, each one higher than the next. A huge wooden post rose into the sky. Noelle shielded her eyes to see a small, round platform on top. A lone sailor was perched there.

*Crow's nest.* That's the word that popped into her mind. Her father had told her . . .

Something occurred to her. Besides the sailor in the crow's nest, there were no others in sight.

"It's really quiet," she commented. "What happened to all of the pirates I saw last night?"

Lenny shrugged. "The sea is calm, so most of them are taking a nap."

"A nap?" Noelle felt a tiny bit disappointed. She had always imagined that the pirates on the Eurastia would constantly be involved in some kind of an adventure. Her nurse's stories had never been about napping pirates.

"So what is Yuri doing?" she asked. "I can't believe a three-hundred-year-old captain is taking a nap, too."

Lenny laughed. "Ha! You're right. I've never seen Yuri take a nap. Also, she probably isn't three hundred years old. Although she's probably older than Karazan."

"Who's Karazan?" Noelle asked.

"He's definitely old—one hundred and one years, exactly," Lenny told her. "He stays holed up in his cabin on the lower deck. We call him Karazan the Prophet."

Noelle shook her head in amazement. "One hundred and one years old," she repeated. She couldn't imagine living so long.

Lenny was heading off again, ready to continue the tour of the ship. Noelle followed him.

"Rumor has it that Yuri drank an elixir of eternal life at the end of the sea," he chatted as they walked. "Did your nurse ever tell you that story?"

"I don't think so," Noelle replied.

They climbed up the ladder to the next deck.

"This is the poop deck," Lenny explained.

Then they climbed one more to the quarter-deck. A young boy was sitting on top one of many large, black cannons. He had jet black hair and black eyes that glittered like diamonds. He was playing a wooden flute.

When he saw Lenny and Noelle, he lowered the flute and smiled.

"This is Zanan," Lenny explained. "He's a pirate apprentice like me. He's a master at playing the Kaylune flute. But he can't talk. His ears are amazing, though. Even when he's doing lookout on the mast, he hears sounds no one else can hear."

"Why can't he speak?" Noelle asked.

Lenny shook his head. "I don't know," he replied. "But when you hear the Kaylune flute, it's easy to understand everything Zanan wants to say."

Zanan picked up the flute, as though he wanted to confirm what Lenny had just said. He put the flute to his lips played a happy melody.

Noelle could feel the music lifting her spirits. She smiled. "That's beautiful," she told Zanan. "Could you please play something for me?"

Zanan stopped the melody. He looked directly into Noelle's eyes.

Then he began to play.

*Ri ri ri, ru ru. Ru ru ri ru ri . . .*

Noelle could almost feel the notes of the quiet melody. They caressed her body like soft strands of silk. The sound was soft and comforting.

But underneath it all was a deep sadness. Noelle could feel that, too.

*Mother . . . Father . . . Where is Johann? . . .*

The song seemed to sink deep into Noelle's heart. She closed her eyes, and a hot tear dropped down her cheek.

Zanan stopped playing. He looked at Noelle with kind concern.

Lenny was flustered. "What happened? Are you okay?"

Noelle's throat was tight, and couldn't answer him. She turned and ran.

Chapter Four:

# Beyond the Waves

Noelle hurried back down the ladder. She didn't know where she was going. She just needed to be alone.

She spotted the rowboats lined up on the main deck. She quickly crouched behind one of them, hiding in the shadows.

"Noelle! Where are you?" Lenny called out. "Noelle!"

His voice faded as he took his search for her to another part of the ship. Noelle let out a deep breath. Then she buried her face in her knees.

*Father!*

The events of that night, a week ago, came flooding back to her . . .

Her mother and father were arguing.

"Someone will betray us," Noelle's mother warned. "The ring has foretold it."

"The servants have been loyal to our families for years," Noelle's father assured her. "How could they betray us? I believe in them more than I believe in this ring."

The kingdom of Ladonia and the kingdom of Odenia had been at war for years. The power of the Zarian Stone Ring had always protected Ladonia. The ring had never steered them wrong.

And this time was no different. One of their servants had betrayed them, just as the ring had shown. Griffith, their most trusted servant of all. All through her childhood, she had spent many hours with Griffith. It was he who taught her how to use a sword.

But it was Griffith who had damaged the Ladonian navy ship and told the Odenian army where to find it. Noelle's father was a master of battle at sea, but weak on land. And that is where the Odenian army had brought him down.

The Odenian army stormed the castle next. Noelle found her mother clinging to life. Her little brother, Johann, was nowhere to be found. With her last ounce of energy, her dying breath, Noelle's mother had given her the ring.

"Noelle, you must survive," she said. "Take care

of Johann . . ."

That was the last time she had seen her family.

Huddled behind the rowboat, Noelle wept at the memory. Then she felt a soft hand on her shoulder.

Noelle looked up into Yuri's face.

"Noelle, are you all right?" Yuri asked.

The pirate captain's voice sounded so much like her mother's. When she was trapped on the black ship, Noelle had kept her feelings bottled inside. She wanted to be strong, to survive. But now they came pouring out. She hugged Yuri and sobbed.

She cried for what seemed like an eternity. When she finally turned her tear-stained face to Yuri, she saw a sad look on the pirate captain's face.

"I'm sorry," Noelle said.

"It's okay, Noelle," Yuri replied. "You should never feel ashamed to cry on this ship. All of us have nowhere on land to go, no place to call home. Everyone on board has shed many tears. Sometimes, crying is the best medicine for the heart."

Yuri covered Noelle's body with her blue cloak. "When you cry so much that it hurts, just look

out at the sea."

"The sea?" Noelle asked.

"In the sea, time doesn't exist," Yuri said. She stood and gazed out at the waters. "Beyond the waves, there is no sadness from the past or pain from the future. There is only now. And now, there is only us, listening to the waves."

Noelle turned to the sea and listened. The waves seemed to be whispering to her, gently soothing her heart. Yuri was right.

She looked up and saw that Yuri was staring intently at the waters. Yuri's eyes seemed as deep as the ocean. Noelle wondered what she was thinking.

After awhile, Yuri turned to Noelle. "The ship is now headed for Pirate's Wharf," she said. "There are people there whom I trust, good people with warm hearts. It will be okay for you to live with them for awhile, until the Odenians stop looking for you."

Noelle knew she would be safe with Yuri's friends. But she had just discovered the Eurastia. She didn't want to leave now.

"Yuri, please let me stay on this ship," Noelle asked her. "I want to be part of your crew."

Yuri looked surprised.

"I don't have anyone on land either," Noelle pleaded. "I'll do anything! I'll even polish the decks! I know a little about using a sword, too. I promise I won't be any trouble."

But Yuri shook her head. "No, Noelle. This is a pirate ship. It's extremely dangerous."

"I don't care!" Noelle cried.

"No," Yuri said firmly. She looked back out at the waves. Her voice softened. "Noelle, when you're on this ship, your time stops. The sea is only for people whose time has stopped. You must not stop your time."

Yuri had nothing more to say. She walked away from Noelle.

Noelle watched Yuri go.

It wasn't fair. She had lost one home, one family, already. She hadn't been on the Eurastia long, but it felt like home already.

She had to find some way to stay.

## Chapter Five:

# King Roden's Castle

Pipps, the merchant, nervously twisted his chubby fingers.

He had shaved his face that morning, for fear of running into Yuri again. But the man he faced now was almost as frightening to him as the pirate girl.

King Roden of Odenia sat in his carved jade throne, glaring down at Pipps. A gold crown topped his white hair, and his dark eyes shone with angry fire.

"So you haven't got the ring!" he fumed.

Pipps bowed so low that his nose nearly touched the red carpet on the floor. King Roden had counted on his army to take down Ladonia. They had succeeded, but failed to capture the Zaria Stone Ring along with the kingdom. Roden had ordered every man in his command to search for the ring.

And then he, Pipps, had found it, had even held it . . . but that hardly mattered now.

"Y-yes, that is true, Your Majesty," Pipps stammered. "We had the girl, too, but before we could leave, the Eurastia . . ."

The king's face colored at the mention of the pirate ship. "Not again!" he hissed through clench-ed teeth. Then he waved his hand dismissively. "That is enough. You may go. Datton! Where is Datton?"

A relieved Pipps hurried out of the throne room. As he left, a tall man walked into the room. His green soldier's uniform was impeccably clean, and his beard was neatly groomed. He stood before

the throne and crisply bowed to King Roden.

"Datton, what is the situation?" King Roden asked wearily. He trusted Datton, the general of the Odenian navy, more than any other member of his court.

"Your Majesty, the Navy followed your orders to head toward the Pentas Islands," Datton explained. "However, we arrived too late. The Eurastia had already escaped."

The general cast a glance back at the door,

scowling. "Also, I feel it is my duty to inform you that the place where the Eurastia appeared was a secret wharf. Pipps was conducting illegal business there."

"I don't care about that!" King Roden snapped. "What I want to know is why an entire navy failed to bring down just one pirate ship!"

Datton held his tongue. Yes, Pipps had lost the ring. But the merchant made a great deal of money for the king. Roden would be forgiving of Pipps, but he expected more from his navy.

"I sincerely apologize," Datton muttered.

"Aren't there a hundred ships in our navy?" Roden went on. "Tell me, why is it that you can't capture one ship?"

Datton planned his next words carefully. The Eurastia was a tricky subject.

"Certainly the number and quality of our ships vastly exceeds the Eurastia. But there is one thing that makes the Eurastia superior," he said, then hesitated for a moment. "It does not sound probable, but that ship has some magical power."

King Roden looked skeptical, yet intrigued.

"What do you mean?"

"The Eurastia moves as if it can predict storms and hurricanes with more skill than any navigator," the general said carefully. "Also, it seems to anticipate my plan of attack, no matter which direction I take. It's like the captain of the Eurastia can see the future."

The king looked thoughtful. He stood up and paced back and forth.

"Datton," he said finally.

"Yes, Your Majesty?"

The king stopped. "I have heard that although the captain of the Eurastia is more than a hundred years old, she still looks like a girl of sixteen. Is this true?"

"It cannot be true, my king," Datton replied. "Such a person could not exist."

"I know that!" Roden said sharply. He shook his head. "Look at me! Every year I grow older. I, the King of Odenia."

King Roden looked directly into Datton's eyes. The general could see the desperation there.

"Datton, this is an order!" Roden said, his voice gruff. "Capture the Eurastia! Bring the captain here with that ring, and we'll force her to tell us the secret of her eternal youth."

Datton suppressed a sigh. Roden had land, power, riches . . . surely such a quest was madness.

"But our men are engaged in battle in—" he began.

"I don't care about that!" Roden shouted. "This is an order, Datton!"

General Datton said nothing more. He bowed to the king, then turned and walked away.

King Roden sank down into his throne. The red velvet curtains behind him shook.

"That was General Datton?"

A man in a black cloak came from behind the curtains. A deep hood hid his face.

King Roden shuddered, as though a cold chill had swept across the room. His mysterious servant was very effective—but his very presence made the king uneasy.

"Yes, that was Datton," Roden replied. "He has been a loyal servant to my family since my brother's reign."

"Ah, so he was a faithful servant to your brother, King Ramden," Black Cloak answered. Roden could hear amusement in his voice. "Your brother was well known, a man born for the people. The complete opposite of you."

A fury rose in King Roden. "Born for the people, you say? He didn't conquer a single island. I am the true king."

"Ah, so that is why you poisoned your brother,"

General Datton said nothing more. He bowed to the king, then turned and walked away.

King Roden sank down into his throne. The red velvet curtains behind him shook.

"That was General Datton?"

A man in a black cloak came from behind the curtains. A deep hood hid his face.

King Roden shuddered, as though a cold chill had swept across the room. His mysterious servant was very effective—but his very presence made the king uneasy.

"Yes, that was Datton," Roden replied. "He has been a loyal servant to my family since my brother's reign."

"Ah, so he was a faithful servant to your brother, King Ramden," Black Cloak answered. Roden could hear amusement in his voice. "Your brother was well known, a man born for the people. The complete opposite of you."

A fury rose in King Roden. "Born for the people, you say? He didn't conquer a single island. I am the true king."

"Ah, so that is why you poisoned your brother,"

said Black Cloak calmly.

Roden looked at Black Cloak with sheer hatred. "Where did you hear that?"

"It is the truth, and you know it," Black Cloak said. "But do not worry. I don't plan to tell anyone."

King Roden's hands began to tremble, and cold sweat poured down his face.

"A man of your age must be careful not to excite himself," Black Cloak warned.

"That will not be a problem for much longer," Roden told him. "Soon I will possess the elixir of eternal youth."

"I regret to inform you that Datton will never capture the Eurastia," Black Cloak told him.

King Roden looked coldly at the man. "Are you saying that you can?"

"Do you doubt me, king?" Black Cloak replied. "Didn't I predict that the child with the ring would be found on Pipps' ship? Didn't I know that the Eurastia would rescue her?"

Roden frowned. He had been warned—but he had not believed Black Cloak then.

"If you do as I say, this time both the Eurastia and the ring will be yours," Black Cloak said, his voice as smooth as honey.

"Can you really succeed?" the king asked, still doubtful. "They say the captain of the Eurastia can see the future."

Now Black Cloak laughed harshly. "She's an ordinary woman. I know her secret. I can outsmart her."

"Her secret?" the king asked.

"Correct," Black Cloak said. "I will capture Yuri for you with my own hands."

Black Cloak turned and walked off, moving silently across the stone floor. But his chilling presence still lingered. King Roden shivered.

"Yuri's secret . . ." he said softly. Then he smiled.

Soon, it would be his.

## Chapter Six:
# Pirate's Wharf

"We're here! Pirate's Wharf!"

Noelle heard the cry from her spot in the middle of the ship, near the main mast. She sat with her back to the ship's hull, trying to stay out of the way. The ship's pirates swarmed the deck, getting ready to disembark. They were all men; some of them as young looking as Yuri, and others, old and grizzled. Their weathered skin was tanned

from days in the sun. Most of them wore breeches, leather shoes and loose-fitting shirts. Every man sported something red in some way or another: a scarf, a shirt, a vest—the color their captain wore.

The sun was just starting to set as the Eurastia sailed into the crowded port. Noelle stared as they approached. Curiosity burned inside her.

Lenny had told her a little bit about Pirate's Wharf after Yuri had said it might be her new home. The village was located on one of the Oum Islands in the southwest Lidenian Sea. Only pirates knew where to find it, and only pirates were welcomed there.

At Pirate's Wharf, these outlaw buccaneers could buy supplies, find treatment for their wounds, and repair their ships. Pirate's Wharf had only one rule: No fighting. It was the only place where captains of rival ships could be seen sitting side by side at the dinner table.

All around Noelle, the excited pirates shouted instructions to one another.

"Don't forget the limes!"

"And the water!"

"Load up on bullets and gunpowder!"

Noelle sulked a little, wishing she could go with them. Yuri wanted her to stay on board until she had made arrangements for a safe new home. Of course, Noelle wanted to stay on the Eurastia permanently. But if she was going to live on Pirate's Wharf, she wanted to see what she was getting into.

Worse than not being allowed off, she wasn't allowed to help on the ship at all. She watched Lenny and Zanan busily carrying empty barrels down to the docks.

I could do that! Noelle thought defiantly. If Yuri could see how useful I could be, she'd change her mind and let me become a pirate apprentice.

Soon the chaos and noise quieted down as the pirates all left the ship and ventured into the village. Noelle watched Yuri and Goa leave last, and resisted the urge to call out.

Questioning Yuri's orders was not the best way to show Yuri she could be a good apprentice. She'd have to sit tight for now.

She sighed and looked out at the wharf. It was nearly dark now, and torches began to spark up one by one, like fireflies.

*Ti-ri-ri . . . ti-ri-ri . . .*

Noelle turned around. She wasn't alone, after all. Zanan was sitting nearby on one of the cannons, playing the Kaylune flute with his eyes closed. Noelle walked toward him.

"You didn't leave with Lenny?" she asked.

Zanan stopped playing and nodded.

"Why?" Noelle asked. "If you stayed behind because of me, please don't worry. I'm fine."

The boy smiled.

"You know, I can be very useful," Noelle said, pouring out all of her thoughts. "I can fence with swords and I'm a fast learner. I know I'd make a

great pirate. So why won't Yuri let me stay?"

Zanan kept smiling, and Noelle suddenly felt embarrassed. Zanan couldn't answer her. So why was she babbling on like this?

"Sorry," she said. "I just wanted you to listen."

Zanan returned the flute to his lips. He played a warm, comforting melody. Noelle sank down at the foot of the cannon, letting the tune wash over her. She suddenly felt less anxious, more content and peaceful.

She looked up at the sky, which had now turned a deep, velvety blue. Stars swirled against this backdrop, forming pictures and patterns. A dazzling white half moon shone in their midst.

For some reason, seeing the stars, Noelle felt the urge to take the Zaria Stone Ring out of her pocket. Its tiny white stars twinkled inside the red stone.

Despite its beauty, Noelle felt a sudden hatred for the ring. It had predicted the deaths of her mother and father. Maybe the ring itself had caused their downfall.

*What if it's some kind of bad luck charm?*

Noelle mused, holding the ring up to the light. *I should destroy it once and for all . . . throw it into the sea . . .*

But something held her back. The ring had been in her family for generations. It was part of her, like the very blood that flowed through her veins.

And for now, it was all she had left of her family.

"Johann . . ." Noelle whispered softly. Not knowing her brother's fate was a terrible feeling. Was he dead? Captured? Lost? Each thought was too much to bear.

She looked at the stone, hoping to find something there that would help her.

*I am a princess of Ladonia,* she thought, staring at the red jewel. *Don't you have any answers for me?*

But all Noelle could see was the moon reflected in the stone's surface. She bit her lip, trying to keep from crying again.

Then the light began to move . . .

The reflection of the moon swirled around the twinkling stars inside the stone. They merged together, like foam on an ocean wave.

The light grew brighter, then transformed before her eyes. The light was forming a picture—almost as though she were looking in a window on another time and place. She studied it.

The stone showed a figure collapsed on the ground. As the image got clearer, Noelle could see a red jacket . . . a braid of golden brown hair . . . a beautiful, lifeless face.

"Yuri!" Noelle screamed.

Chapter Seven:

# Karazan's Prophecy

Horrified, Noelle watched the scene inside the stone continue. She saw herself run up and grab Yuri. Men surrounded them, their swords drawn . . .

The sound of the Kaylune flute startled Noelle. The flute's cry sounded urgent. She quickly tucked the ring in her pocket.

"Zanan, what is it?" she asked.

Zanan jumped off of the cannon. He ran to the hatch that led to the ship's lower decks and opened it.

"Wait!" Noelle cried. She ran after him.

Zanan climbed below several decks, making his way down ladder after ladder until he finally stopped. The air smelled damp and musty; Noelle realized they must be in the very bottom of the ship.

She followed Zanan down the dimly lit passage to the very last cabin. Zanan opened the door, and they both stepped inside.

Like Noelle's cabin, this space also held only a hammock and a small table. An old man sat in front of the table in a wheelchair. Long, white hair streamed down his back and from his chin. Deep wrinkles lined his thin face. He wore a light blue cloak over his frail shoulders.

The old man was frantically ringing a small bell.

"Is someone here?" he called out.

In reply, Zanan blew softly on his flute.

The man silenced the bell, and looked up at

Zanan. Both of his eyes were clouded over with a milky white film. He was blind.

*He must be Karazan, the one hundred and one year old pirate Lenny told me about,* Noelle realized. *He's certainly the oldest-looking person I've ever seen.*

"What's wrong?" Noelle asked.

Karazan looked startled at hearing her voice. "Who are you?" he asked.

"Noelle," she replied. "Yuri saved me."

Karazan drew closer to Noelle. He placed both hands on her face. His milky eyes seemed to stare right through her, although she knew he could not see.

Noelle strangely felt light-headed. She struggled to focus as Karazan spoke in a low voice, almost like a chant.

"Noelia," he began, and Noelle almost gasped. That was her given name, the name she used in the court of Ladonia. "You will overcome many hardships," the old prophet was telling her, "then an age of peace will come . . . a new future . . . but with this peace will come the loss of a friend."

Noelle sank to her knees, exhausted, although she wasn't sure why. Karazan removed his hands from her face. His voice was crisper and he looked more alert, as though he had woken up from a dream.

"Why did I ring that bell?" he asked himself. "Oh, yes. I have something important to tell Yuri. Please fetch her for me, quickly."

"Captain Yuri just left the ship to go to Pirate's Wharf," Noelle told him.

"Oh dear. It's too late then!" Karazan wailed.

"What's wrong?" Noelle asked.

"Yuri cannot go to Pirate's Wharf," the old man said darkly. "Something evil is waiting for her there. A monstrous black shadow. Yuri's injury makes it impossible for her to see it herself. But I have seen it. Yuri will perish!"

The image of Yuri's lifeless body flashed into Noelle's mind. The Zaria Stone Ring had foreseen Yuri's end. And now, so had the prophet Karazan.

The ring must have shown the truth. That meant Noelle was in danger as well.

Noelle's heart began to beat quickly. She should flee . . . escape . . . run far away from the ship, listen to the ring. Her father hadn't listened, and now he was dead.

But if she did that, then Yuri would surely die. Yuri, who had saved her life.

Noelle took the ring out her pocket and stared into the stone.

*To save myself, I must abandon Yuri,* Noelle thought. *But I can't do that. She saved me.*

Noelle felt a tap on her shoulder. She turned.

Zanan pointed at himself, then pointed to the small porthole in Karazan's cabin. The lights of Pirate's Wharf burned in the distance.

She grabbed the boy's arm to stop him.

"No," she told him. "I will find her."

Zanan shook his head. But Noelle stood her ground.

"The ring has shown me what will happen," she said, looking into his eyes. "I have to try to change that."

Zanan gazed intently at Noelle for a moment. Then he slowly nodded.

"If you're going, go to Mousehole Road," Karazan told her. "Yuri will definitely be with Majobaba. Her house is at the end of the road. But hurry!"

"Got it!" Noelle replied.

Then she ran.

## Chapter Eight:
# Majobaba

Noelle ran through the cobblestone streets of Pirate's Wharf. She pushed her way through groups of pirates making their way in and out the rickety wood buildings that housed taverns, fortune tellers, doctors, and shops selling spices, food, and weapons.

The pirates here were not as clean and friendly-looking as the mates on the Eurastia. Their clothes were filthy, their beards were unshaven, and most of them smelled like rotten cheese. She tried to slip through their ranks unnoticed. Even though she was in a hurry, she was too afraid to ask one of them for directions to Mousehole Road.

Fortunately, Noelle didn't have to look far. There was one main road, and she followed it until she came to a narrow back street. No torches lit the way here, so she bravely ran into the darkness.

Each house on Mousehole Road was more run-down than the one before. Some were wood shacks, worn by the sun and torn by summer storms. Others were made of crumbling stone.

Noelle reached the last house on the block and stopped. Its stone walls looked as though they had been slapped together. The stone steps leading to the front door were breaking apart.

*Can Yuri really be here?* Noelle wondered.

The front door seemed locked, and the shutters on the first floor windows were all closed. Noelle thought about knocking on the door, but hesitated. What if she were in the wrong place? What if she was too late? She shivered.

Then she spotted some barrels piled up on the side of the house. She looked up and saw light shining through one small window.

*I'll have a look first, before I knock,* she told herself. She climbed the shaky barrels, moving slowly to keep her balance. Then she peered through the window.

She looked down into a small, clean room. It felt warm and welcoming, compared to the outside of the house. Light flickered from a gas lamp on a small table. A pot bubbled on top of a black stove.

And there was Yuri sitting upon a stone platform in the center of the room. Goa stood silently by the door.

Just then, the door opened, and an old woman entered. Her long, gray hair shone like silver in the lamplight. She walked to the stove and picked up the steaming pot. Noelle could now see that a strange, green liquid bubbled inside.

*What is she doing to Yuri?* Noelle wanted to scream, but found herself frozen in fear and wonder.

The woman gently pulled up the back of Yuri's shirt. Noelle gasped.

An angry red wound stretched across Yuri's pale skin. It looked fresh.

The woman touched the wound with her wrinkled fingers, and Yuri's shoulders trembled.

"It's deeper than before, isn't it?" Noelle heard the old woman ask with a sigh.

"The stone can stop time, but it cannot heal this wound," Yuri answered with sadness in her voice.

The woman scooped some of the pasty green liquid out of the pot. She patted it onto the wound, shaking her head.

"Yuri, when I first met you, I was an apprentice. It was my teacher who dressed your wound for you," she said. "That was seventy years ago. I'm an old woman now, but you're exactly the same now as you were then. Your time has stopped."

She covered the entire wound with the paste. Then she returned the pot to the stove. She wiped her hands on a rag, then turned and looked at Yuri. Her dark eyes were grave.

"It is against nature to stop time, Yuri. Your wound grows deeper every day," she said. "The medicine helps. But if you keep using the stone like this, the wound will eventually destroy your body."

"I know," Yuri replied, and her voice sounded tight and tired. "But there is something I must do."

After a few minutes, the green liquid dried. The old woman carefully scraped it off. The wound looked less red and swollen—but it was still there.

Yuri climbed down from the stone platform. Suddenly, ten children barreled through the door. They circled Yuri, chattering with excitement.

"Yuri! Yuri!"

"When did you come?"

Noelle watched, curious. Some of the children looked as though they had just learned to walk; others appeared to be teenagers, like Yuri. They all looked clean and happy.

Yuri smiled at them. "I just got here. Majobaba gave me some medicine."

A little boy with curly hair ran up and hugged Yuri's legs. "Hey, I can read stars now!" he boasted.

"I'm not surprised. You're a smart little boy, Luda," Yuri told him.

A little girl held out a rag doll to show Yuri. "Look, Yuri! See the clothes on this doll? I made them!" she said proudly.

Yuri picked up the doll and studied the clothes. "Wonderful, Rena!" she said. "You will make a great seamstress some day."

A tall boy stood next to Yuri. His face beamed with pride. "Yuri, I'm going to be an apprentice at the glassblower's shop on Belze Island."

Yuri squeezed his hand. "That's terrific, Sedi!"

The old woman laughed. "Yuri is tired, children. And it's time for you to sleep."

Luda frowned. "But I still want to talk to Yuri!"

"Yuri will visit again," Sedi told the little boy. "Now kiss Yuri good night."

One by one, the children kissed Yuri. She smiled as she watched them go.

"Everyone's doing well," Yuri remarked.

"Yes," the woman said, nodding. "They are wonderful and they are all so helpful."

"Majobaba . . ." Yuri began. "Actually, there's another child I'd like you to look after."

Noelle held her breath. Yuri was talking about her.

"Of course," Majobaba said, without hesitation. "I'd take in anyone you brought here. What is she like?"

"She's eleven," Yuri said. "She's quite pretty. I heard her cry for help . . ."

Noelle leaned forward so she could hear better. Then she heard another voice—but this one was rough, and came from the ground below her.

"The house is completely surrounded."

"We've got men stationed in the trees across the street, as you ordered," came the reply from another deep voice.

Noelle peered into the darkness below. A group of men were gathered there. A tall man in a black cloak stood in the center of them.

"Good, hold your positions," Black Cloak said. His deep voice filled Noelle with fear. "Don't move until Yuri leaves the house and crosses the street. Then—we will attack!"

Chapter Nine:

# Ambush!

Panic swelled up inside Noelle. She had come to warn Yuri—but she'd hesitated, she'd eavesdropped instead, and now she was too late!

"What should we do about the man called Goa? There's a rumor that he's immune to bullets," one of the men asked Black Cloak down below.

"Don't worry," Black Cloak replied.

Noelle, atop the barrels, clung to the side of the

house, holding her breath. If they saw her now, there would be no hope at all.

Through the tiny window, Noelle watched Yuri hand a bag of coins to Majobaba. "Thank you," Yuri told her.

"No problem," the old woman replied. "Bring that girl anytime."

Yuri walked toward the door and nodded to Goa. Thoughts clashed in Noelle's mind. Should she cry out in warning? Then the men would storm the house. She thought of the children . . .

Noelle heard the front door of the house creak open. Yuri would cross the street next. She had to do something, But what could she do? She had no sword to fight them with, just the empty barrels under her feet.

Down below, the men stepped out of the shadows, led by Black Cloak.

*I've got do something!*

Noelle reached up to the shingled roof over head. She gripped it tightly. Dangling, she kicked at the empty barrels with all of her strength.

They tumbled to the street with a huge crash.

Startled, the men turned, pointing their weapons toward the loud noise. One of the men let off a shot. The sound exploded in the quiet night air.

In the street, Goa shielded Yuri with his body and drew his cutlass.

Noelle swung herself up onto the roof. "Yuri! They're in the trees, too! Run!" she yelled.

Black Cloak turned and looked up.

"Catch the girl!" he cried. "She's on the roof."

Two men hurried back toward the house. Noelle ran to the center of the roof.

Down below, others aimed their weapons at Goa. Incredibly, bullets bounced off his body as though he were made of armor.

Men in black, who'd been hiding, jumped down from the trees, their swords drawn. Yuri broke away from her first mate and faced them. Her cutlass moved swiftly in the moonlight as she slashed at her attackers.

Then Noelle heard a grunt. Two men had climbed to the roof. She looked around. Where could she go?

Then she spotted the roof of the next house. It

was the same height as the one she was on now, but about five feet away.

She had no choice. Noelle took a deep breath. She ran across the roof, stepping over the arm of one of Black Cloak's men. Then she pushed off the roof as hard as she could.

Terrified, her stomach plummeted as she soared through the air. Oh, no! She had come up short. Frantically, she reached out with both arms.

*Whomp!* She managed to grab the roof's edge. Heart pounding, she pulled herself up.

Black Cloak's men had the same idea. They charged across Majobaba's roof after her.

Noelle saw the roof on the next house. She had to keep moving. Maybe she'd get lucky, and her pursuers would slip up and fall.

She ran and took off again. This time, she landed squarely on her feet. But as her feet touched down, something warm stung her shoulder. A sword. She'd been hit. The shock caused Noelle to lose her balance, and she plummeted to the ground below.

"Noelle!" Yuri cried.

The fall knocked the air out of her lungs. She moaned, feeling a patch of soft sea grass beneath her. It must have broken her fall.

"Sir, we've got her!"

Noelle looked up to see two of Black Cloak's men staring down at her. They each grabbed an arm and pulled to her feet.

Goa let out a battle cry and charged toward Noelle's captors. But after three steps he stopped in his tracks, dropping his cutlass. He covered his ears, crying out in agony.

Black Cloak, holding a black box, stepped in front of Goa. Noelle could hear a soft humming sound coming from the box.

Yuri paused and stared at Black Cloak. Her face turned pale.

"It can't be . . ." she stammered.

Black Cloak laughed.

"That's right," he said. "This device can shut down Goa's artificial brain. It has no effect on humans, but it causes robots to stop functioning. Goa's useless now."

Yuri was breathing heavily. Several of Black

Cloak's men surrounded her but her cutlass was drawn, ready to finish them off.

"Come, throw down your weapon," Black Cloak urged her. "If you don't, I'll kill the girl."

Black Cloak nodded toward his remaining henchmen. They left Yuri and surrounded Noelle, their swords drawn. Goa fell to the ground like a freshly cut tree.

"Yuri, don't do it!" Noelle cried. If she did, the vision in the ring would surely come true. They would both be lost . . .

*Clang!*

Yuri dropped her cutlass. She glared at Black Cloak.

"Tell me who you are!" she demanded.

## Chapter Ten:
# Yuri's Secret

Black Cloak's evil laugh rang through the street like a bell tolling doom.

"Have you forgotten me, Yuri?" he asked, placing the box inside his cloak. "We worked in the same laboratory, after all."

The moonlight softly shone on Yuri's rigid face. "It can't be," she said softly. "You died in the explosion."

"I almost died," Black Cloak said. He slipped off his hood to reveal a face twisted with thick, white scars. Noelle gasped in horror.

"You did this to me!" he cried angrily. "And selfishly, you kept the stone. The one thing that can help me."

Black Cloak was consumed by his hatred for Yuri, lost in it. Noelle saw an opportunity.

"Yuri, forget about me and run!" she yelled.

Black Cloak turned and smiled thinly at Noelle.

"Such noble words. But do you know the whole story, little girl?" he asked. "Do you know what your precious captain did?"

Noelle gazed at Yuri, and saw the pirate captain's face was as pale as the moon. Yuri would not look at Noelle.

"Yuri comes from the future," Black Cloak told her.

Noelle let this sink in. Was Black Cloak telling the truth, or was he mad?

"I don't believe you," she said.

"She worked in a science lab with her father,"

Black Cloak said, ignoring her. "They created stones that can shrink and expand time—the Timelight Stones. The power of the stones is terrifying."

Black Cloak turned and stared fiercely at Yuri as he finished the story. His voice was sinister. "The energy of the stones is difficult to control. There was a great explosion—an explosion that destroyed half of the world. Yuri was one of the lucky ones. A layer of time cracked open, and she and Goa were sucked through it and brought here, a thousand years in the past."

His voice grew louder and more filled with hate. "Don't you understand, little girl? Yuri wiped out half of the world and only saved herself! Now she's traipsing around as a pirate captain. That's what kind of person she is."

Yuri closed her eyes and softly shook her head.

"That's a lie!" Noelle shouted. "Yuri would never do that! She couldn't . . ."

Her voice cracked and then faded. She had trusted Griffith, too, hadn't she? She had known him her whole life. And yet Griffith had betrayed her and her family. She'd lost her mother, her father, her whole country.

Sometimes people weren't what they seemed to be. Noelle stared at Yuri. Could it be true?

"Little girl, this is the truth about the pirate captain you love so much," Black Cloak said. He pointed at Yuri. "You can turn yourself into some kind of crime fighter if you want. But you can never undo what you did."

Yuri sank to her knees and stared at the ground. Black Cloak slowly walked toward her, step after silent step.

"Give me the stone," he said.

Yuri clenched her fists.

"No," she said, and her voice was shaking. "I won't give it to you."

"And why not?" Black Cloak asked.

Yuri looked up at him. A faint fire gleamed in her eyes once again. "Because you plan to use the power of the Timelight Stones for yourself. That was your plan in the future, wasn't it? Why would that be any different now?"

"There's nothing wrong with using the stones,

Noelle cried. "I won't give it to you or

oak grinned. "Think hard about this,
f I have that ring, I can make the Time-
es. I can combine the power of the stones
back in time. I could bring your parents
life. Save your country from the Odenians.
all that for you, in exchange for the ring."

trange feeling came over Noelle, as though
est of the world had frozen around her. Yuri,
men, Majobaba's house—they all faded away.
wasonly aware of Black Cloak's words, which
hoed in her mind.

"My parents . . . alive," she whispered. "And
ohann . . ."

Was it really possible? Noelle knew the ring had
power. And everything Black Cloak had said about
Yuri—it all made sense now. The rumors about her
age. Goa's inhuman strength. It had to be true.

Then the power of the rings was true, too. Black
Cloak could bring back her family. He could save
the people of her country.

"Noelle, you can't believe anything this man

Yuri," he replied, and his voice was almost hyp-
notic. "We created them. We are bound to use their
power. Look."

Black Cloak removed a chain that hung from his
neck. He held it out to Yuri and she saw that a
locket hung from the chain—a locket with a bright
green stone. Yuri was shocked.

"But the Green Stone exploded . . ." she said.

Black Cloak laughed. "Of the three stones, only
the Red Stone exploded. You have the blue. The

green is in my hand. That's why you couldn't see my image in your blue stone. The Green Stone's power protected me."

Black Cloak slowly circled Yuri now. "How about it, Yuri? Why don't we join forces once again? Together we can make a new Red Stone. Then the three stones will come together once more. If we do that, we can move freely through time. Just think. We can rule the universe!"

The Timelight Stone he held began to glow with an eerie green light. In response, Yuri's stone flickered with blue light. She held the stone tight, though her hand was shaking.

"No thanks," she said.

"What did you say?" Black Cloak snapped.

Yuri stood up. "I became so obsessed with the stones that I was blind to the idea that someone might use them for the wrong reasons," she told him. "Because of that, something terrible happened! The only reason I continue to live on this earth is so that I can find a way to destroy the stones I helped to create."

Black Cloak's eyes burned with anger in his

scarred face. "...ll that's true, ...
way," he snarled. He raised ...
turned as one and point...

Noelle broke fre... from ...
them, heading straig... at Y...

"Stop!" she screame...

Black Cloak roughly ...
stumbled, and the Zaria St...
pocket and clattered onto the ...
eyes grew wide.

"The Zaria Stone Ring," he ...
heard of it, but never seen it with m...
stone from which all three Timelight ...
made."

Noelle quickly snatched up the ring an...
back on her feet, wondering, what did Black ...
mean?

"With the Zaria Stone, I could make all ...
Timelight Stones I wanted to," he went on, hi...
eyes gleaming. "You must be the daughter of the Ladonian lord. The girl who escaped Pipps."

Noelle took a cautious step backward.

"Give me the ring," Black Cloak commanded.

"Never!" ...
to anyone!" ...
Black Cl...
little girl. ...
light Ston...
to travel ...
back to ...
I'll do ...
A s...
the r...
the ...
She ...
ec...

says," Yuri called out.

But Yuri's voice sounded like the buzzing of bees in Noelle's ears. As if in a trance, she slowly walked toward Black Cloak.

"You will do it?" she asked Black Cloak. "You will bring them back to life?"

Black Cloak nodded.

"You have to promise me," Noelle said. "Promise me I will see them again."

"I will," Black Cloak said solemnly.

"Noelle, no!" Yuri begged.

Noelle heard her this time, but she did not listen. She didn't want to.

"Here," she said softly.

Then she placed the Zaria Stone Ring in Black Cloak's palm.

### Chapter Eleven:
# The Power of the Rings

Black Cloak stared at the ring in his hand. He began to laugh.

"I don't need your stone anymore, Yuri," he said. "I have all I need now."

"What about your promise?" Noelle asked. "When can I see my parents?"

Black Cloak's mouth formed a twisted grin. "Would you like to see the power of the stone? I will show you now."

He raised the stone high in the air. A beam of green light shot from his hand like a lightning bolt.

"Look out!" Yuri cried. She bounded toward Noelle and tackled her to the ground.

The lightning passed just over the top of Noelle's head and hit the tree behind her. Noelle heard a strange groaning sound and looked back. The tree was aging before their eyes. Within seconds all the leaves fell off, and the trunk split in two. The wood inside was dry and decayed.

"What a pity," Black Cloak said. "Just a little closer and I would have turned the little girl into a wrinkled old woman."

Yuri sprung to her feet, ready to fight Black Cloak. But he raised his hand again, and another beam of light shot from the ring. Yuri ducked, and the light hit a stone wall. The wall crumbled and turned to sand in an instant.

The horrible reality of what she had done roused Noelle, as though she were waking from a dream.

"Monster!" Noelle screamed. "You deceived me!"

"You were wrong to believe me," Black Cloak cackled. He hurled another beam of light at Noelle.

She closed her eyes.

*I am finished*, she thought. *There is no escaping him. And it is all my fault . . .*

She braced herself for the impact, but nothing happened. She opened her eyes.

Yuri had aimed a blue light from her locket at the green beam. The two lights collided in mid air, sending sparks shooting into the night with a crackling sound.

Then the light beams melded together, forming a curtain of light, a shield between Black Cloak and Yuri. Black Cloak was furious.

"How dare you try to stop me!" he fumed.

The surge of anger caused the green light to grow stronger. Yuri staggered, but held firm. Her face was twisted in pain. She was sweating profusely.

Then Noelle noticed something. Blood dripped from the bottom of Yuri's red jacket. The wound had opened up again.

Majobaba's words to Yuri came flooding back to her.

*If you keep using the stone like this, the wound will eventually destroy your body.*

"Yuri, you can't use the stone!" Noelle cried out. "You'll die!"

Yuri turned to Noelle, her face pale.

"Noelle, run!" she said hoarsely.

"But Yuri—"

"Don't worry about me," Yuri said. "Run. Now!"

The green light became even stronger, and Yuri staggered backward. Black Cloak laughed.

"Your stone has power, Yuri, but don't forget— I have the ring now," he gloated triumphantly.

He held the ring up next to the locket in his right hand. Red light shone from the Zaria Stone Ring, giving power to the green Timelight Stone.

The green light was so bright now that Noelle had to shield her eyes.

"This is the end, Yuri!" Black Cloak cried.

The green light spiraled toward Yuri, sizzling as it shot through the air. It sliced through the blue light, surrounding Yuri's body. She cried out in pain, unable to defend against it. Then she collapsed.

"Yuri!" Noelle screamed.

Then a shot rang out.

The green light instantly disappeared. Black Cloak groaned and lowered his hand, dropping both the locket and the ring.

Another light glowed brilliantly on the street now—the light of dozens of torches. Men and women carried them, and surrounded Black Cloak and his men. Their clothes were worn and dirty, but their eyes gleamed fiercely. Each torch-wielding person also bore an old sword or pistol.

"There is one rule on Pirate's Wharf. No fighting. Got that?"

Majobaba stepped out of the crowd. Smoke rose from the pistol in her hand. She pointed it directly at Black Cloak.

Black Cloak bent down and picked up the locket. The green stone had cracked, and only a dim light burned inside it now.

"It's useless to me now," he said. "But the ring

. . . where is the ring?"

"Are you looking for this?" Majobaba asked. She held out her palm. The red stone glittered in the torchlight.

"What are you fools doing?" Black Cloak barked at his henchmen. "Grab the ring!"

The people of Pirate's Wharf sprung into action before Black Cloak's men could react. The henchmen drew their swords, and the sound of metal clashing filled the air.

Noelle ducked behind one of the townspeople

and picked up Yuri's cutlass. The blade felt heavy in her arms. She stood in front of Yuri's fallen body, ready to fight.

One of Black Cloak's men charged toward her, a small dagger in his hand. Noelle raised Yuri's cutlass above her head. She brought it down with a mighty blow, knocking his weapon to the ground.

"Captain! Noelle!"

Noelle turned quickly to see Lenny and Zanan running toward her. Behind them, the crew of the Eurastia charged into the fray. They raised their voices in a loud battle cry.

Black Cloak's men were clearly outnumbered. Black Cloak glared at the pirates in frustration.

"This isn't over yet, Yuri!" he cried. "Next time we'll settle things once and for all."

He pushed past two of his men and quickly fled. His panicked henchmen followed, disappearing into the night.

The townspeople raised their torches, cheering.

"We did it!"

"We got them!"

But Noelle felt no sense of victory. She knelt

by Yuri, searching for some sign of life. The pirate captain wasn't moving. Her skin felt as cold as ice.

"Yuri, don't die!" she begged.

## Chapter Twelve:
# Lights in the Darkness

"Yuri!"

Majobaba pushed her way through the crowd. She pulled Noelle off of Yuri and put her ear to Yuri's heart.

"Her breathing is steady," the healer said after a moment. She turned to the crowd and called out, "Get a stretcher! Bring Yuri to my house as fast as you can!"

Noelle was amazed at how quickly the townspeople came to Yuri's aid. Two men appeared almost magically, carrying a stretcher made of two wooden poles. They carefully lifted Yuri onto the stretcher. Then they quickly carried her to Majobaba's house.

Noelle followed and, once inside, watched the men lift Yuri onto the stone table. Majobaba looked at Noelle.

"Do you want to help?" Majobaba asked.

Noelle nodded.

Majobaba spoke to the townspeople who had begun to crowd into the room. "Everyone, please go home. You'll just interfere with Yuri's treatment if you all stay."

When they cleared out, Majobaba shut the door tightly. She took off Yuri's red jacket, then gently lifted the shirt from Yuri's wound. Bright blood oozed from it now.

"Yuri!" Noelle cried.

"Yuri needs you to stay calm, Noelle," Majobaba whispered. She walked to the stove and began the work of creating a new poultice for Yuri. She started with a pot of clean boiling water. Noelle watched as the old healer added pieces of dried green herbs from stalks hanging on the wall. She stirred the whole mixture with a wooden spoon. Then she nodded to Noelle.

"Keep stirring," she told her.

Noelle stirred and stirred. Finally the medicine began to thicken. Majobaba first grabbed a bottle of clear liquid from a shelf. She applied it to the wound with a rag.

"To help the pain," she said simply.

Then it was time to spread the green medicine once again over the wound. Yuri groaned in pain. Noelle grabbed her hand.

"Yuri, hang in there," Noelle whispered.

The green liquid once again dried into a thick paste.

"Is Yuri okay?" Noelle asked worried. The pirate captain's face still looked so pale, and her hand felt cold in Noelle's.

"The bleeding has stopped," Majobaba told her. "She should be fine."

Majobaba was right. Soon, the color returned to

Yuri's face. She grew much calmer, and fell into a peaceful sleep.

Noelle dabbed the sweat from Yuri's face with a clean cloth. Then she noticed that Yuri was clenching something tightly in her hand.

Majobaba noticed it too. She gently pried Yuri's fingers open, revealing the blue stone locket. It shone with a dim light.

"The stone . . ." Noelle whispered. She had witnessed its amazing power not long ago. It had all seemed unreal.

"It is the Timelight Stone," Majobaba said. "Yuri's eternal youth, her strange power, and her pain are all because of this stone."

"So is Yuri really from the future?" Noelle asked.

Majobaba did not answer. She picked up the medicine pot and carried it back to the stove. Then she walked back to Noelle.

"You have a wound on your shoulder," she said. "Let me see."

Majobaba examined it for a moment, then took another bottle of liquid from her shelf. She began to dress the wound.

"I don't know where Yuri came from, and I don't care to know," the old woman said quietly. "What's important is what she's doing now."

When she finished, Majobaba walked to the window and opened the shutters. The townspeople had circled the house, still carrying their torches.

"They're still worried about Yuri," Majobaba said. "I'll go tell them she's all right."

She lifted up the gas lamp and waved in front of

the window. The townspeople saw the signal. A jubilant cheer rose up.

"The people who live on this street have all lost the lives they once had," Majobaba began, staring out the window. "They were all cast aside, their homes and their families taken from them. They felt they had no reason to live. Only Yuri believed in them. She brought all of them here, and thanks to her they found the strength to go on. I help her with that."

Majobaba turned and peered into Noelle's eyes. "The people she brought here don't care what rumors they hear about Yuri," she said. "They know the kind of person she is, and that's all that matters."

Noelle cast her gaze out the window. Each torch was proof of someone's love for Yuri. There were so many people . . . and Yuri had saved all of them. Just like she had saved Noelle.

"Yuri carries a heavy burden," Majobaba said. "But she never blames anyone for it and never tries to cast it off. I can help her, but I can't make her burden any lighter. All I can do is . . . believe in her."

Majobaba reached into her skirt pocket.

"I'll return this to you," she said. "It's yours, isn't it?"

The Zarian Stone Ring glittered in her palm. Noelle accepted it from her with a trembling hand. If what Black Cloak said were true, this ring would create the Timelight Stones a thousand years from now.

"Yuri asked me to take care of you, but after what's happened, it won't be safe for you to stay here," Majobaba decided. "You should stay by Yuri's side. Try to believe in her, if you can. That's the only thing that can help her."

Yuri moaned quietly. Noelle walked to her and gently touched her shoulder.

"Yuri . . . Yuri," Noelle said.

Yuri slowly opened her eyes. "Where am I?"

"You're in Majobaba's house," Noelle told her.

Majobaba handed Yuri the shining blue locket. "You must take this," she said. "Your voyages are not over yet."

Yuri's eyes filled with tears. Noelle knew how she must feel. The stone had been the cause of so much pain. It would be, again.

Yuri took the locket from Majobaba's hand. The color had returned to her face.

The door slowly creaked open.

"Yuri, are you okay?"

It was little Luda. The other children crowded behind him, peering into the room. Majobaba grinned.

"Yes, I think she'll be okay," she told them.

The children whooped, and jumped for joy. Luda rushed in and clung to Yuri's arm. The other children did the same.

Yuri hugged each and every one of them. "Don't worry about me," she said. "I'm fine."

"But Yuri, we thought you died!" Luda said. A fat tear rolled down his cheek.

Yuri looked like she might cry, too. She hugged Luda even tighter.

Then the house became noisy with hurried footsteps. Lenny and Zanan appeared in the doorway.

"Captain, are you all right?" Lenny asked. He was out of breath.

"Yes, thanks to Majobaba," Yuri replied.

Lenny looked relieved. Then his expression turned serious as he gave Yuri his report. "Black Cloak's gang—we followed them but they escaped quickly. Also, there was no sign that their ship had left. But it's nowhere to be found on the island."

Yuri gazed out the window, thoughtful. "It's okay," she said after a moment. "I'm sure we'll meet them again sometime."

Then the pirate captain grabbed the handle of her sword and stood up, using her sword like a cane. She stumbled a little, and Noelle rushed to her side. Yuri smiled.

"Thank you, Noelle," she said.

The deep sound of a conch shell sounded from the wharf. Yuri looked at Lenny, Zanan, and Noelle.

"The Eurastia is called," she said brightly. "Come! We need to start our voyage."

Chapter Thirteen:
# A New Journey

Noelle stood on the captain's deck, staring out into the sea. The light of the moon danced on the waves.

Everyone but the lookout in the crow's nest was fast asleep. The only sound she heard was the gentle crashing of the waves.

*Splash . . . splash . . . splash . . . .*

Noelle thought about what Yuri had told her.

*Beyond the waves, there is no sadness from the past or pain from the future.*

"Noelle?"

Yuri stood in the doorway of the captain's cabin.

"Yuri, how are you feeling?" Noelle asked.

Yuri smiled and walked toward Noelle. "I'm fine. And I think Goa's brain will start working again, too."

The moonlight shone on Yuri's face. Her dark eyes looked peaceful, but Noelle thought she could see a sadness there, deep inside.

"Yuri . . ." There were so many things Noelle wanted to say. She just didn't know where to start. She took a deep breath.

"Yuri, I'm sorry," she began. "If I hadn't given the ring to Black Cloak . . ."

Yuri said nothing for a while. She stared at the sea. Then, slowly, she began to speak.

"I'm the one who should apologize to you," she said. "Everything Black Cloak said . . . it's true."

Yuri let this sink in. Noelle's mind reeled.

"A thousand years into the future, I unleashed

the power of the Zaria Stone. I was able to extract the particles of light within the stone that are able to control time. I crystallized them to create the three Timelight Stones. I was able to use the stones to warp space and time.

"Can you imagine how much power I had?" Yuri went on. "I was convinced it was a power that could be used for good. But both my father and I became obsessed with our discovery. This obsession led to conflict and disagreement . . ."

Yuri's voice wavered. She looked up at the moon.

"The Timelight Stones exploded because of that conflict. I grabbed the Blue Stone. Then Goa and I fell a thousand years into the past," she told the story.

Noelle reached into her pocket and felt the Zaria Stone Ring. It was incredible to think that this very same ring would cause so much damage a thousand years from now.

"Yuri, what if I throw the ring away?" Noelle asked. "Then I can prevent what happens in the future, right?"

Yuri shook her head. "Even if it falls to the bottom of the deep sea, a thousand years from now, someone will find it and the same thing will happen."

"So what should I do?"

Yuri tenderly grasped Noelle's hand. "Noelle, it's my job to figure out a way to destroy the Zaria Stone," she said. "As its current owner, it's your job to take good care of it. That's all."

Yuri looked back out over the waves. "Until I

can destroy the power of the stone, I'll continue drifting over the sea. My time will remain stopped."

She turned to Noelle. "We're not far from a small port town. The Odenians don't know about it, so you'll be safe. I want you to get off the ship when we arrive there."

"Please, no," Noelle said.

"Don't worry," Yuri replied. "I've arranged it so that you can live there safely."

"Yuri, please don't do this," Noelle begged.

"My time has stopped, but yours hasn't," Yuri said firmly. "I can't let you join someone like me, sailing endlessly across the sea."

But Noelle was not going to give up. "No, Yuri," she said, her eyes burning with determination. "I'll follow you no matter what you say. My father didn't believe in the stone. He believed in people. That's why he died. I thought my father was a fool."

Noelle took a deep breath, trying to remain calm. She had to convince Yuri. "Now I understand," she said. "For my father, it was important to trust people over something like a stone. That was the way my father lived."

Noelle looked into Yuri's eyes. "I believe in people, too. I don't care about the past or the future. I believe in the Yuri of now."

Yuri didn't reply. The deck was quiet once again, except for the sound of the waves.

*Splash . . . splash . . . splash . . . .*

Yuri smiled.

"Thank you, Noelle."

There was a sound of soft footsteps behind them. Lenny appeared.

"Hey, Noelle, where have you—" He stopped when he saw Yuri.

"Am I interrupting something?" he asked.

"No, Lenny, you're just in time," Yuri answered. She put her hand on Noelle's shoulder. "Let me introduce you to our new pirate apprentice, Noelle!"

Noelle let out a happy gasp. Lenny looked shocked. Then he grinned.

"Really? So Noelle's one of us now? Yes!" He shook Noelle's hand. "Glad to have you on board,

Noelle!"

Lenny pulled Noelle across the deck. "Come on! Let's tell everyone the good news!"

"But they're all asleep!" Noelle protested.

"Doesn't matter. Come on! Let's go!" Lenny urged.

Laughing, Noelle followed him.

Yuri smiled as she watched them go. Then she turned back to the moonlit water.

*Splash . . . splash . . . splash . . . .*

Somewhere, beyond the waves, Black Cloak was waiting. Yuri grasped the locket tightly in her hands.

When they met again, she would be ready.

# Afterword

In its original Japanese, *The Pirate & The Princess* is called *Pirate Girl Yuri*. It contains elements of both science fiction and fantasy.

The character of Majobaba is like a fairy godmother figure one might find in the world of fantasy. To heal Yuri's wound, Majobaba brews a mixture of herbs into a medicinal green liquid. Anyone who has read Andersen's *The Little Mer-*

*maid* is likely to recall the scene in which the sea witch brews a potion for the mermaid who has fallen in love with a human prince and asks to be made human. To brew the potion, the sea witch throws various ingredients into a pot. Unlike the sea witch, Majobaba does not use magic; she simply brews a medicine to cure a wound. And yet the wound was caused by the strange power of the Timelight Stone, which means her medicine was anything but ordinary.

From the novel we know that the Timelight Stone has the strange power to freely manipulate time and space, something we are unable to accomplish using today's science. However, scientists such as Albert Einstein have developed theories supporting the idea of time travel. It's possible that 1,000 years in the future, these ideas will be made real.

In this story as well, the reader is surprised to discover that Yuri was hurled back in time from the future to the fairytale world of the past. In this sense, this novel is classic science fiction.

The Timelight Stone is a simple device with

amazing powers. Even though the stone was created in a science lab, it has magical properties. In this way, the book combines science and magic to tell a story.

By the way, even though the main character Yuri is a pirate, she's nothing like the fearful one-legged men in Stevenson's *Treasure Island*; she's a noble young girl. This alone makes the story unique. However, because she created the Timelight Stones, which caused so much destruction, Yuri bears a huge burden.

Noelle, who was saved by Yuri, lives with the tragic memory of her parents' murder and the takeover of her country. Noelle is also the owner of the Zaria Stone, the parent of the Timelight Stone. For this reason, Noelle carries a burden no less heavy than Yuri's. And yet Noelle rejects Yuri's offer to live a safe life and chooses instead to join Yuri in her "voyages without time," becoming a member of the Eurastia.

Another theme of the book is wandering on the sea. These two girls must now face Black Cloak, who wants to use the Timelight Stones to control the universe; and the Odenian King Roden, who wants the Zaria Stone Ring for himself. What thrilling adventure will the girls face next? Let the next amazing battle and adventure begin!

# SNEAK PEEK!

And now, here's a preview of the continuing
adventures of Captain Yuri and Noelle in
the second book in the series . . .

THE PIRATE AND THE PRINCESS

The Red Crystal

Chapter One:

# The Calm Before the Storm

*Sailing the ocean waves . . . searching for treasures . . . helping people in danger . . . cutlasses clashing . . .*

Noelle's mind wandered, thinking of all the stories she had heard as a child. The life of a pirate sounded like the most exciting thing in the world.

She dipped her coconut brush in a pail of cloudy water. In the six months Noelle had been a pirate apprentice, she had done a lot of things. She learned how to repair the sails and she took care of the ship's pigs and cattle. She had peeled more potatoes than she could count. And she had scrubbed the deck. Scrubbed, and scrubbed, and scrubbed. Noelle rubbed the brush against the wood planks of the deck. The sun warmed her back, and she swept her brown hair away from her face.

Being a pirate apprentice was not nearly as exciting as she'd imagined—it was hard work! But she didn't really mind. If it meant she could be a pirate like Yuri some day, it was all worth it.

Besides, she had friends to help her. Lenny and Zarnan were both apprentices, too. They scrubbed the planks alongside her.

Today, Lenny, however, was fed up.

"I am sick and tired of this!" he said. He threw down his coconut brush in disgust.

Noelle kept scrubbing. "Yuri's going to be angry with you, Lenny," she warned.

Zarnan nodded but didn't say a thing. The boy couldn't speak.

"I don't care," Lenny said stubbornly. "For

three days now, we've been scrubbing the deck. I can't stand it!"

Noelle understood her friend's impatience. Lenny had been a pirate apprentice since he was five years old. He could climb the ship's mast faster than any sailor on board. It frustrated Lenny to be stuck in one place.

"There's nothing we can do about it," Noelle told him. "There's no wind and there are no other jobs to be done."

"Forget it," Lenny said. "I'm not holding a brush

anymore, no matter what!" In protest, he flopped down on his back, his arms and legs spread out wide.

Noelle grabbed Lenny's hand and tried to pull him up.

"Come on, get up!" she urged. "You're going to get a good scolding if she finds you like this."

But Lenny didn't move. "It's okay. Look at them."

He nodded toward the other side of the deck. The other pirates had become listless under the lazy afternoon sun. One man was fast asleep and snoring. Another stared blankly as he twisted an old piece of rope.

Noelle sighed. Her favorite stories had been about the pirates of the Eurastia. Her nurse had described Yuri's men as brave and strong. Noelle had always pictured them all as tall and handsome. This ragtag bunch of men on the ship couldn't possibly be Yuri's dashing crew, could they?

Lenny held up his palms. "See, Noelle? My hands are so full of blisters that I can't hold a brush anyway."

Noelle cocked her head and narrowed her eyes. Lenny's hands were red, but she didn't see any—

"—Blisters? My goodness!" came a chuckle from behind.

Noelle whirled around. "Yuri!" she cried.

Yuri had an amused smile on her face. She hardly looked like the fierce pirate captain who made villains quake in their boots. But Noelle knew just how strong Yuri could be.

"Scrubbing the deck may be boring but it's an important job," Yuri said, gently but sternly. "If mineral deposits form on the deck, it can get slippery and dangerous. So be sure to get it all off."

Lenny quickly picked up his brush. "Yes, Captain!" he said loudly. "You can count on me!"

Zarnan laughed and Noelle just shook her head. She had warned Lenny, hadn't she?

"That's more like it," Yuri said, smiling. "You seem to be have a perfect grasp of that brush— your *blisters* aren't getting in the way at all."

She turned to Noelle. "You've become quite accustomed to the ship," Yuri remarked.

"She may be used to the ship but you should see her when she tries to act like a pirate," Lenny teased. "Nothing like a princess at all—ow!"

Noelle playfully smacked Lenny on the head. She had been a princess once—that was true. But just because she was a princess didn't mean she wasn't tough. She knew how to handle a sword, after all.

Yuri laughed. "You're right, Lenny. She may turn out to be a great pirate."

Noelle blushed. Through all the hard work of the last six months, she had never complained. She'd gotten blisters on her hands—real ones. There were times her body had hurt so much she couldn't get out of bed. But now she could climb the mast and lower the sails, just like a real sailor, and she had never been more proud of herself.

But today the sails hung limply from the mast. "Yuri, isn't the wind going to blow again?" Noelle asked. "We've been here for three days."

"We can't control the wind, Noelle," Yuri replied. "We have plenty of food, so there's nothing to get anxious about. Let's just relax and wait.

Nature will do the rest for us."

Noelle gestured toward the crew. "But if there isn't any wind, even their brains are going to melt."

Yuri checked out the lethargic pirates and chuckled. "That's true. Well, shall we put a little fighting spirit into them? Lenny, please go to the armory and bring back the biggest bow and arrow."

Happy to be temporarily relieved of scrubbing, Lenny jumped up and quickly ran away. He returned with a bow and arrow taller than he was.

Yuri took a white handkerchief from her pocket. From her other pocket, she extracted a gold coin. She wrapped a gold coin in the handkerchief and then tied the little package to the arrow. Then she faced the mast, which looked like a flagpole, and took aim.

*Twang!* The arrow flew up and pierced the main mast just above the crow's nest. The sound of the arrow got the attention of the pirates. They turned and looked at Yuri.

"There's a gold coin tied to that arrow," Yuri

announced, pointing to the top of the mast. "Whoever can reach it, can keep it. Who wants to try?"

"I do! I do!" the pirates cried. They all dashed off toward the flagpole.

Lenny, as always, was faster than all of them. He hopped on the head of a short, fat pirate. Then he shimmied up the pole like a monkey. In seconds he was within reach of the arrow.

"That gold is mine!" he shouted triumphantly. He reached out his hand . . .

*Bang!* A pistol shot rang out. The arrow split from the mast, then dropped to the deck below.

Garanan, a one-eyed pirate, waited to catch it. Noelle knew he had the best aim on the ship.

"Yahoo! That gold piece is mine!" Garanan cheered.

But before he could catch the arrow, something reached out and intercepted it. Noelle saw that it was a hand and arm carved out of wood.

Holding the arm was a pirate with a mustache and wire-rimmed glasses. Demir was the inventor of the ship. He pressed a button and the arm came back toward him, powered by a spring.

"My new extendable hand worked!" he said proudly.

But the thin arm was too flimsy to hold the large arrow. It cracked and broke.

"I knew it! Demir's inventions always fail!" one of the pirates called out.

A bunch of pirates rushed to grab the arrow as it fell to the ground. Something silver glinted in the sun. Romesu, a master swordsman, had swiftly cut off the handkerchief that held the coin. It dangled from the tip of his sword.

"The coin is mine, now," he said, grinning.

"Look again, Romesu," said another pirate. Dominos was a short man who wore a silk hat taller than the length of his head. "The one you have is a fake. The real one is here."

The magician took a handkerchief-wrapped package from under his hat. Romesu frowned and opened the package on the end of his sword. There was no gold coin inside—just a piece of wood.

"Bravo!" Noelle called out. That was a pretty good trick!

Dominos bowed. "Thank you. And now, happily, the gold coin is—"

"Think before you show off," a crewman called out. Bino, the spear master, threw a wood spear across the deck. It pierced the handkerchief, taking it right out of Dominos's hand.

Unfortunately, the spear kept flying—right over the side of the boat!

"Oh no!" Bino cried. He ran to the rails, followed by the other pirates. Noelle dashed after them, too.

The spear bobbed on top of the waves. They could all see the gold coin was still attached—but it was out of reach.

*Splash!* Someone dove off of the deck into the water. A head of brown hair emerged from the waves. It was Zarnan!

"Zarnan! Get back here!" one of the men yelled.

"It's not just the flute he's good at," Noelle pointed out. "He's a great swimmer, too."

"Yeah, he swims like a seal," Lenny agreed. "Hey wait, where's he going?"

Noelle strained to see. It looked like Zarnan was swimming away from the spear.

"Hey, Zarnan, the coin's not there. It's the other way!" someone yelled.

"To the left! To the left!" the crew called out.

Zarnan ignored them. He kept swimming. Noelle could see a barrel bobbing up and down in the water.

Yuri had been laughing, but suddenly, her face

grew serious. She grabbed the telescope that dangled from her waist and looked through it.

"Demir, Garanan, lower the lifeboat!" she shouted. "Follow Zarnan!"

"What's wrong, Captain?" Garanan asked.

"Someone's out there!" Yuri cried. "There's a man hanging onto the barrel! Hurry!"